The Magic of
Marionettes

Anne Masson

Cover photo by Anne Jane Grieve
A special thanks to the students of Beaverton Public School

Edited by Sandra Bogart Johnston
Design & graphic realization by Monica Charny

Distribution in Canada and the USA:
Firefly Books Ltd.
250 Sparks Avenue
Willowdale, Ontario
M2H 2S4

Printed in Canada
by Maracle Press

Canadian Cataloguing in Publication Data

Masson, Anne.
   The magic of marionettes

ISBN 1-55037-042-1

1. Puppets and puppet-plays—Juvenile literature.
I. Kinney, Pamela.   II. Title.

PN1972.M37 1989   j791.5′3   C89-093008-2

TABLE OF CONTENTS

To Hercules Smart and his daughter,
Muriel Anne, who taught me the value of
looking for and encouraging creativity and
individuality in children of all ages.

Acknowledgements

A book is never written by just one person. It takes many different thoughts and ideas, and much encouragement, to complete a work of this nature. Thanks for years of support to Mom and Dad. Thanks to my sisters, Jan and Nancy, who added their memories to these pages. And thanks to Grandpa Hercules, without whom all of this would never have started.

The final touches before sending a manuscript off to a publisher are the most difficult to accomplish. My heart and soul had been in this manuscript for more than ten years, but nobody really believed I could make it into a real book until Murray. His technical skill and loving encouragement to "Go for it!" helped me to make my dream a reality.

There couldn't be a better publishing company than Annick. To Rick and Sandra, thanks for your part in my magic.

The Marionette

A marionette is "a doll or puppet moved by strings," according to *Webster's Dictionary*. The word actually originates in the France of the Middle Ages. The term came from religious plays called "Les Mystères," which were performed in front of cathedrals. Originally both people and doll-like figures were the actors in these plays. Later just the puppets were used, and nicknames given to the little characters. The favourite character in the plays was often Mary, the mother of Jesus, and the nicknames for the puppets came from her name. "Les Petites Maries" gradually became the short form "Les Mariettes," or "Les Mariottes"—the former was used by the townspeople while the latter was popular among the peasants.

Through the process of linguistic evolution in France, the name changed from Marie to Marielle, Mariolle, Mariotte, Mariette, and finally to Marion, eventually producing the diminutive, Marionette. This French word was adopted by the Italians during the Renaissance, and applied to their string puppets. The English language has formally accepted the Italian use of the word, while the French use it for any type of figure appearing in an animated show.

Earliest picture of medieval puppetry is this 12th-century woodcut.

About This Book

This book is for all those who have felt the magic of a marionette at some time, and thought they'd like to get more involved, but were afraid to try. I was lucky. My Grandfather saw how fascinated I was with marionettes on television (Topo Gigio on *The Ed Sullivan Show*, I think it was), and he brought me one from Mexico. From that simple beginning my collection has grown to over thirty marionettes. My sisters and I, as children, along with some of the neighbourhood kids, used to put on puppet shows in our basement. My Dad, Ed, built us a stage which I still use today, and my Mom, Muriel, spent hundreds of hours listening to our countless rehearsals and meetings.

Courtesy of the Ontario Puppetry Association

When I began teaching I used my marionettes as a teaching tool, and soon we were making them in art class and putting on shows for the rest of the school. Their magic is abundantly clear in the classroom. The magic takes old torn newspaper, flour-and-water paste, wire and costumes, and transforms them into an artistic masterpiece. The magic takes that otherwise uninterested child who hates everything about school, and makes him or her into a star.

Each person who makes a marionette will spend a long time doing so, and during that time will discover ideas, and form creations, that may look less than perfect to the uninvolved observer, but that nevertheless have been painstakingly pondered over and carefully executed. The purpose of this book is not to help create a perfect marionette by professional standards, but to help children—and adults too—explore their creativity in a new medium, and to instill pride in that accomplishment. Girls ease their tension about hammers and saws. Boys discover they can create with a needle and thread. The magic inspires them all.

The stage directions and performance hints are to be handled in the same way. The point is not to have the very best play ever written or performed, but to create a play produced by the whole group—even those who don't often succeed at everything. It's important to have the children excited about the project, and not afraid to offer suggestions or to try out new ideas and techniques.

Wherever the play is performed, whether it be in the living room for relatives, or in the school for teachers and students, it will be appreciated and admired as a performance created by the children themselves. I have also worked at home with children on marionettes. It's a great project for children as young as five for quiet activity, a super opener for casual non-threatening discussion time, and a wonderful long-term project for rainy weekends, or summers.

The directions, I hope, are easily followed, with room left for lots of individual creativity, which I hope you'll share with me. If you see something you think might work as an alternative, please try it and let me know of your successes.

As you read through the book I hope some of its suggestions will inspire you to create a little magic of your own.

—Anne Masson

Where to Start

This book covers various aspects of the world of marionettes—creating the puppet itself, putting on a performance, writing a play for the marionettes to perform in, plus one sample play. You might want to write your play first, and then make puppets based on the characters you've created. It is, of course, possible to make the puppets first, but usually the first question children will ask is, "What should I make?" With a play already written, the question can be narrowed to, "Which character in our play do I want to make?"

Or, if you want to launch right into puppet making, you could create a puppet based on a character in the sample play, or use a character from an existing play, a favourite story, or a fairy tale. Choose whichever route appeals to you, and jump right in!

Courtesy of the Ontario Puppetry Association

Creating the Basic Human Puppet

Building the Head

You will need:

a) For the papier-mâché:

- old newspapers

- flour: 750 mL (3 C) altogether, but mix only 125 mL (½C) at a time

- cup and spoon for mixing

- water

b) For the head:

- thin wire (made from peeling the paper off twist ties or from unbent paper clips)

- scissors

- a lightweight round or ball shape as the basis for a head (a balloon partially blown up, a styrofoam ball, pantyhose containers, a ball of wool, wool pom-poms, a sponge ball, an old tennis or ping-pong ball, a stuffed old sock, wooden macramé beads, a ball shape formed from old newspaper)

To make the papier-mâché:

Tear the newspaper into 1 to 2 cm (½ to 1 inch) pieces and collect them in a bag.

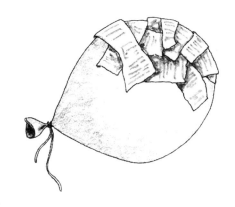

Make paste from the flour and water: To 125 mL (½ C) flour add enough water so that it looks like gravy. Soak paper pieces in the paste for at least 10 minutes before using them—they must be really wet and gooey.

Put one layer of papier-mâché on the puppet head and let it dry thoroughly. (Find a safe, well-ventilated place to leave the head, away from little children, pets, or anyone who might mistake the glob for garbage and throw it out!)

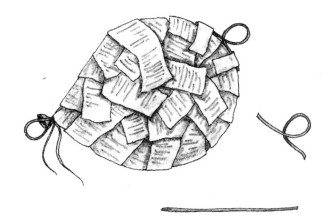

Cut the thin wire into 5-cm (2-inch) lengths and make three loops. Attach them to the head with tape, and put another papier-mâché layer over the whole head. (The wires are important because they will hold the whole marionette together, so make sure they are very secure.) Let the head dry again.

Add one more layer of papier-mâché, getting the surface as smooth as possible, then let dry.

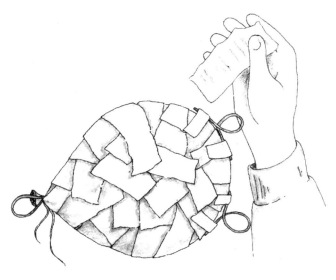

When the head is a suitable shape, add features. For the eye, make a wad of wet papier-mâché the size the eye is going to be. Attach it in the appropriate place and plaster papier-mâché over it, using the bits of wet paper like tape.

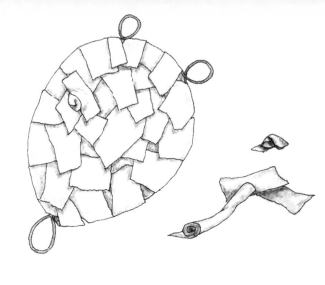

Using the same technique, create other features—the other eye, the nose, lips, ears, chin, beard, eyebrows, and so on. This part can get very slippery. If the head gets too wet and pieces start to fall off, try doing one feature at a time and letting it dry for awhile, then move on to another feature. Remember to keep the "skin" as smooth as possible. Make each feature quite large and distinctive—larger than it would be in real life—so that when the head is painted the features will be clear to the audience.

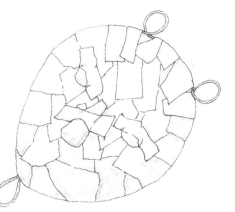

HINT: If the paste begins to get smelly while parts of the head are drying, try adding a little soap to the paste (either dishwashing or laundry) to keep it smelling fresher.

Building the puppet head will take several days and require drying time in between. Materials for costumes and props can be collected during the drying time. A sewing box can be a treasure trove of bits of material, rickrack, bows, pins, scraps of felt, wool, buttons and so on. Look in a tool box as well—nuts and bolts, or wires, might be useful. Collect anything that is even remotely useful! (Even orange juice cans, inverted, make great puppet hats. Be imaginative!) A shoe box makes a great collecting box for your costume and prop materials.

Painting the Head

You will need:
- water colour or acrylic paint, or an inexpensive paint box set

- a paintbrush

Use bright colours and make the features slightly exaggerated, so the audience will be able to see the details. Eyes are most effective if you use three colours. If water colours are used, spray on acrylic after completion to keep the colours from running—a couple of layers of hair spray works well.

Building the Body

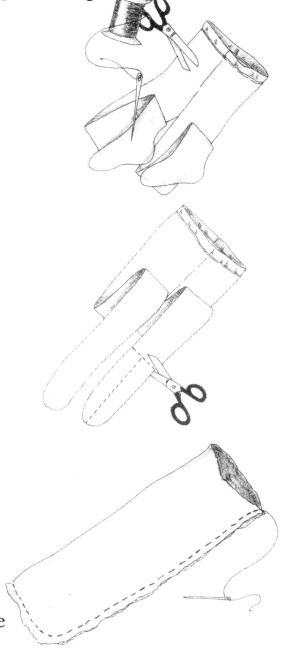

You will need:

- about three pairs of old panty hose

- a needle, thread, scissors

Cut a 12 to 15 cm (5 to 6 inch) length from the pantyhose foot, for the puppet's legs. Then cut that piece in half lengthwise. (Cut the second pantyhose foot in the same way, to use for the puppet's arms.)

Sew along the length of the cut piece, but keep the top open. Stuff the piece with bits of cut-up pantyhose. (Use the parts near the waistband, because the lower leg or calf area will be used for the puppet's body.) Sew up the end. Don't worry about seams showing— they will be hidden when the puppet is dressed.

Make a knee joint by sewing across the middle of the leg. Repeat for the other leg, making sure the seam for the knee is the same distance up the leg. To make arms, repeat again with a shorter piece of pantyhose (9 to 10 cm or 3½ to 4 inches). Make the elbow joints the same way as the knee joints.

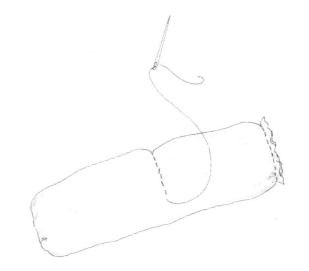

Cut off a 12 to 15 cm (5 to 6 inch) length of pantyhose for the body. Sew the bottom seam, and stuff the piece, then stitch the top seam.

Sew the arms and legs to the body.

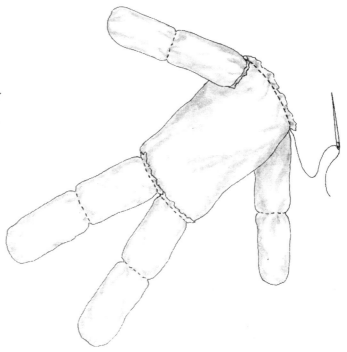

Sew the head to the body with strong thread, using the wire loop at the base of the head.

To Make Hands

Mitts can be easily made and fitted over the ends of the arms. Use the puppet's arm as a base for the size of the mitt, and trace a simple pattern onto the material chosen. Felt works well for this because it can be glued instead of sewn, but any firm fabric will do.

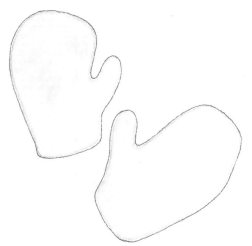

A more elaborate hand can be made by shaping the hand and fingers from wire, and covering with felt or material, or even papier-mâché. Be sure to add a wire loop at the base of the hand so it can be sewn onto the arm.

A big, floppy hand for a clown can be made by cutting the shape from felt and sewing it to the end of the arm.

To Make Feet

Any kind of small shoe, such as a doll's shoe, can be used as a puppet's foot. Just attach it to the bottom of the leg.

If you knit, or you know someone who can, a small knitted slipper looks terrific.

Old baby booties or shoes are fine too, if you can find some small enough. Or, shoes can be made from pieces of felt, and sewn or glued together.

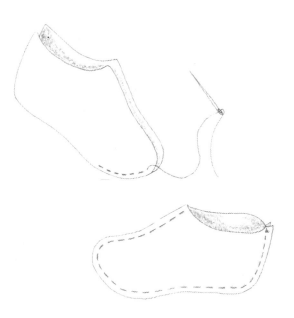

Dressing the Puppet

Now the body is ready to be dressed. Handmade clothes or doll's clothes can be used. If these aren't available, check out your box of collected costume and prop materials. Remember that soft fabric that will drape well usually works best, and try to leave the arms and legs clear of too much fabric.

COSTUME HINTS

• Costumes that are lined usually hang better.

• If costumes don't hang well, insert small weights into the hems and edges of the costume. This can be particularly effective with cloaks and trains.

• All parts of the costume should be made with large arm holes, and large necklines and waistlines, to allow for freedom of motion.

• Costume jewellery is handy for crowns or other details.

• Keep the costume fairly simple.

Character Ideas

Imagine a rock star, an athlete, or a T.V. personality. Take a look around. Make a satirical character out of someone you know, or maybe a football star...how about hockey or baseball?

Perhaps your interests lie in outer space. Create a space explorer. When you're making the head from papier-mâché, add bumps here or lumps there, enlarged ears or a cone-shaped head, one (or three!) eye sockets, a peculiar nose, and so on. At the same time mold on unusual hair (mohawk, fluffy, punk). Let your imagination soar with the costume—a silver lamé suit, a cape from shiny or metallic fabric, high boots, etc.

Whatever ideas you come up with will be great. Add a string here or take one away there. It's your creation, so go for it! Ideas can be collected from all kinds of sources. Sometimes an interesting piece of material or leftover sewing notions will suggest a character. You could make wonderful clown hair from wool, wiry pot cleaners or raffia.

Remember there are no wrong answers or bad ideas. Let your imagination guide you.

Courtesy of the Ontario Puppetry Association

Courtesy of the Ontario Puppetry Association

Courtesy of the Ontario Puppetry Association

- cardboard and aluminum foil can make crowns and swords

- try using fancy seam binding for necklaces

- key chains that have miniature shoes and telephones can be used for clothing or props

- try knitting scarves, hats and other items for your marionette

- pipe cleaners make excellent eye glasses

- add rick-rack to your clown's ruffles

- drapery rings can also be used for belts and bracelets

- any scraps of fancy material can be used for capes, or dresses

Creating the Basic Animal Puppet

Make the body pieces in the same way as for a person. (See pages 14 to 16.) Just make the arms the same length as the first pair of legs, and put them together differently, in an animal shape. You can also make the whole body out of papier-mâché, the same as the head.

Heads

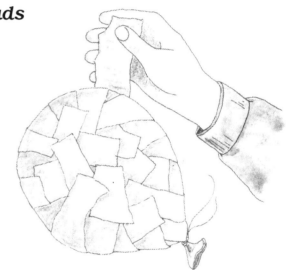

Try using a partly blown-up balloon for the head. It can be made to suit various animals, depending on which way the balloon is facing—fat end forward for a kitten or a lamb, pointed end forward for a mouse, fox, or anything with a long snout. Make the head using the balloon, papier-mâché and wire loops, using the instructions for the basic puppet head (on page 11.) The three head loops are in basically the same positions as on a human puppet, but the head will sit horizontally rather than vertically. Attach the loops while applying the papier-mâché, as you do on the human puppet head.

Animal Bodies

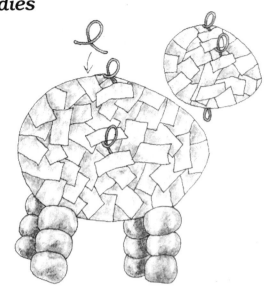

There are three extra loops required on the body of an animal. Sew the body loops on if the body is made of stuffed pantyhose, or if the body is made of papier-mâché, attach them to one of the first layers.

Sew an extra joint for a foot, just as you did the knee, if you're not adding a separate foot.

Leg Variations

Almost anything can be used for animal legs, especially fantasy animals. Try stringing beads (wooden or plastic beads, or macramé beads), or try some colourful vinyl rope with a weight at the bottom. A bead or piece of weighted styrofoam works well. Long hollow wooden pieces from young children's bead stringing kits make great poodle legs, with some fur or wool attached.

You can make beads from papier-mâché by forming balls around straws. Four or five layers of papier-mâché make a good-sized bead, and the straw (which is later removed) creates a hole for the beads to be strung on.

Did You Know That...
Well-preserved marionettes have been found among the relics of ancient Egyptian tombs.

For another variation, make traditional wool pom-poms and use them as leg pieces, strung together like wooden beads. This technique can also be used to make a great long neck for an ostrich or giraffe. Use your imagination!

Pom-Pom Instructions

You will need:

- cardboard

- scissors

- wool

Cut two doughnut shapes from cardboard, about the size you want the finished pom-pom to be. Place the two pieces together.

Wind yarn or wool around both pieces of cardboard, until all the board is covered and the hole is completely filled.

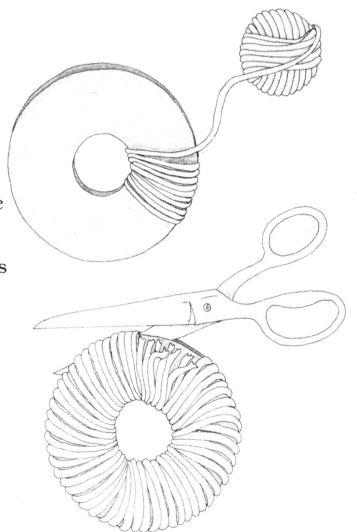

Cut the wool carefully between the two pieces of cardboard. Then tie the wool very tightly in the centre, with a matching piece of wool, between the cardboard pieces. Carefully remove the cardboard and *presto!*—a pom-pom.

24

Tails

The tails can be made in the same way as the bead legs, but the individual pieces should be smaller. You can use a tube-shaped wooden bead from a bead stringing kit as the long part of the tail, then add a wool pom-pom, a ball of fake fur or a larger round bead at the end.

For a horse's or cow's tail, a small piece of rope frayed at the end, and dangling freely, does the trick.

A rabbit's tail can be a pom-pom attached to the rump with a very short piece of wool.

For a great pig's tail just twist a piece of wire in a curl and attach it to the pig's rump.

For a reptile like an alligator or crocodile, make a multi-sectioned tail out of pieces of papier-mâché hooked together with wire loops. When it's suspended from the tail string it will appear to slink along the stage floor.

Did You Know That...
Marionettes were used by travelling showmen in the Middle Ages because there was no radio or television to tell people about news and events.

Ideas for Animal Marionettes

Dogs

Imitation fur makes a good covering for a dog's body, or for a French poodle, pom-poms. A sheepdog looks good made from wool tassels which have been frayed to make them fluffy. Just sew them all over the body until the dog looks shaggy enough.

Cats

Cats can be done in much the same way as dogs. For Siamese cats a velvety material can be used, with buttons for eyes, broomstraws for whiskers, a pink velvet material for ears—maybe a pink tongue too. Fluffy kittens look good made from pom-poms.

Birds

An ostrich is a great idea for a marionette because of its tall, gawky shape. Styrofoam balls covered with feathers make fine bodies and heads.

(An old Christmas decoration made from a styrofoam ball, and covered with silk threads, makes a terrific bird's body.) Try some plastic rope for the legs and neck, felt for the beak— and even for the long eyelashes! Or, a combination of styrofoam balls and wool pom-poms is good. If you use a balloon for the body and cover that with papier-mâché, you can paint it or cover it with feathers. Use pipe-cleaners for some of the animal's features—like eyeglasses.

Elephants

Make the trunk and ears from wire. They can be either regular size, or giant Dumbo size. Cover the wire shape with papier-mâché, and use more to attach the ears to the head, formed over a partly inflated balloon. The legs can be regular beads, or beads made from papier-mâché formed over a straw, rope or nylon.

Did You Know That...
The main difference between marionettes of the Orient and those of Europe was their temperament. Oriental marionettes were gentle and shy. Western marionettes were grotesque and satirical.

Monkeys

Monkeys are made almost the same as people. Try using darker pantyhose for the body, arms and legs. Just add a curly wire tail—maybe even put a bell on the end! You can dress the monkey in a vest or a funny shirt, and add a hat or pants, but leave it barefoot.

Snakes

Make a snake body from pantyhose, either full-width or half, depending on the snake's desired size when compared to the other marionettes in the show. Attach strings to the head and body, but skip making any legs. The snake will not be as complicated as other marionettes to operate.

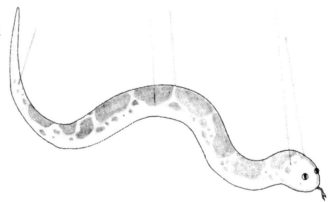

Did You Know That...
In Europe during the 3rd or 4th century AD, puppeteers used to travel from town to town performing the Nativity story on small stages built on the back of covered wagons. The stringed puppet that portrayed Mary was called "little Mary" or "Marionette," and that is, of course, the same term used today to refer to all puppets operated by strings.

Building the Operating Sticks (Human)

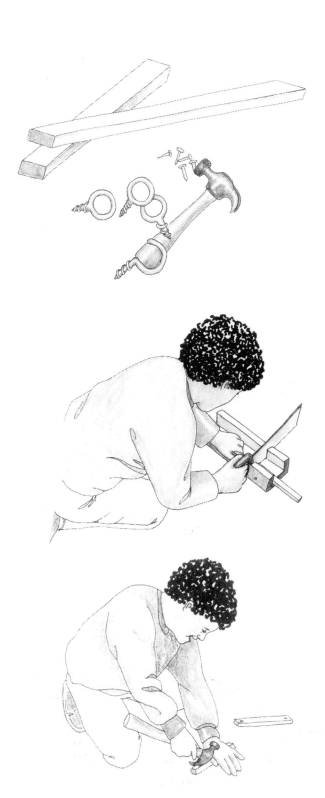

You will need:

- about 30 cm (1 foot) wood. The best kind is 1.5 × 2 cm (½ × ¾ inch) wooden dowelling, but any kind of squared-off wood will do.

- three eyehooks

- one cup hook

- several fairly thin nails (twice the depth of the dowelling or sticks) and a hammer

- a hand saw and mitre box if the wood is not pre-cut

Cut the wood to make two pieces about 15 cm (6 inches) in length.

Using the hammer and a nail, put holes in each of the four ends of the wood, about 1.5 cm (½ inch) from the ends. (Hammer the nail in and pull it out again, leaving the hole.) (Keep the holes a little way in from the very end of the stick, so the wood won't split. If it does, you can fix it with a little white school glue and an elastic band.)

Nail the two pieces of wood together in the middle, and screw the cup hook into the top of the top stick as shown. Insert one eyehook at the front end of the top stick, on the underside. Insert two eyehooks 4.5 cm (2 inches) from the middle of the lower stick, on the underside.

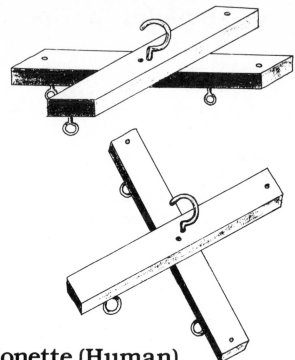

Stringing the Marionette (Human)

You will need:

- strong thread or string (black, blue, red and yellow helps you keep track of which string is which, but you can use all one colour; fishing line or dental floss can be used instead for added strength)

- a needle and scissors

- a ruler

Someone to hold the marionette while you string it is a great help!

To keep these instructions from getting too complicated, it's easiest to colour the diagram. Colour the head strings black, the back string yellow, the foot string (going from one foot up through the two eyehooks on the lower operating stick and down to the other foot) blue, the hand string (going from one hand up through the front eyehook and down to the other hand) red. The colours simplify the operation of the marionette during a show, for if several marionettes are in a scene it is difficult to see what they are doing, from the operators' top view. (Pulling the blue string always means that the feet are moving, etc.) However, you can use all one colour if you wish.

Begin with the black head strings. Lay the puppet on the floor or on a table and place the sticks about 45 cm (18 inches from the head. Measure two pieces of black string, longer than you need. (The whole marionette, including strings, should be about 75 to 85 cm (30 to 34 inches) tall in order to fit properly on the stage.

Tie one string to the loop at the side of the head, then to the outside hole at the same side of the lower stick. Repeat for the other side.

Tie or sew the yellow back string at the back of the waist, well hidden in the puppet's clothes, if possible. Take it up to the back hole of the top stick and tie it.

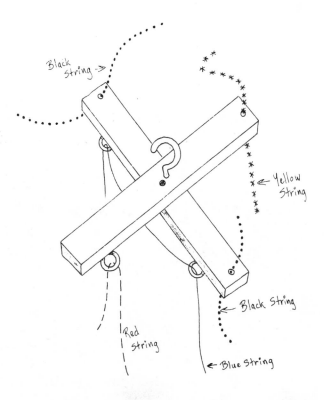

For the blue leg strings, cut **one** long string. Tie the string to one knee. From here go up through the two eyehooks in the lower stick, then back down to the other knee. Adjust to match the head and back strings—the puppet should hang straight from the strings, without back or knees bent. Tie.

Cut **one** long red string for the hand strings. Tie one end to one hand. Then go up through the eyehook at the front of the top stick, and back down to the other hand. Tie.

Did You Know That...
Italy has the most interesting marionettes. They are found in every province, and they vary in form and operation in each locality just as the dialects do.

Building the Operating Sticks (Animal)

Note that the operating sticks for an animal puppet are different than for a human puppet. The cross stick for the leg and foot strings is the same, but the head and tail stick, which will be the top operating stick, is longer— about 18 cm (7 inches) total.

You will need:
- 30 cm (1 foot) piece of 1 × 2 cm (1/2 × 3/4 inch) dowelling, or other wood

- 4 eyehooks

- the same materials as for the regular operating sticks (see page 29)

Cut the dowelling into two pieces, 18 cm and 12 cm (7 and 4³/4 inches).

Make holes near the end of each piece of wood. Add another hole halfway along the bottom of the long stick, and another a quarter way along the long stick.

Screw in the four eyehooks. Join the two sticks as you did the regular operating sticks, and add the cuphook at the top.

Stringing the Marionette (Animal)

Begin with the red head string. Attach one long red string to one loop at the side of the head, go up through the front eyehook on the operating stick, and back down to the loop at the other side of the head. Tie off. The string should be long enough so the marionette (including strings) is approximately 75 to 85 cm (30 to 34 inches) tall.

Now tie the black back string to the loop in the puppet's back, and go up to the eyehook near the back of the longer stick. Tie off.

The blue leg strings are tricky because in order to assure easy and lifelike manoeuvring, the legs are strung diagonally: that is, the right front foot is attached to the same string as the left back foot.

For the right front foot and left back foot:
Start with one blue string, a bit longer than the height of the marionette (including the strings). Tie to the eyehook at the right end of the short operating stick—the *puppet's* right-hand side. Take the string down through the loop on the right side of the head (the red string is already there), continue to the puppet's right front knee or foot. Tie off. Now take a

slightly longer piece of blue string and tie it to the *same* eyehook on the operating stick. Take it down through the same head loop, then continue across the puppet's back, through the left loop on the side of the puppet's body, and to the back left knee or foot. Tie off.

For the left front foot and right back foot:
Now do the reverse for the left front foot and right back foot! Tie a blue string to the operating stick eyehook on the *puppet's* left side. Go down through the loop at the left side of the head, and tie the string to the left front knee or foot. Begin again at the *same* left side of the stick. Tie a slightly longer blue string to the eyehook, and take it down through the left loop on the head. Then cross over the puppet's back to the loop on the right side of the body. Go through the loop and down to the right back knee or foot. Tie off, adjusting length to be the same as the opposite blue string.

For the tail simply tie a yellow thread to the back hole in the long operation stick and to the tail. Leave the yellow string a little slack, so that the tail can dangle freely and move naturally even if it is not being moved intentionally. For some tails, such as a horse's or cow's, you don't need to attach a tail string at all unless you specifically want to create movement in the tail.

If you create a creature with many legs, like an octopus or spider, or an unusual shape like a space creature, don't be afraid to add more strings to make your animal or creature work properly.

Hints for storage and Display

Marionettes are always fastest to use when they're hanging up. Try to avoid laying a marionette down for storage—the strings always end up tangled, and untangling marionette strings can be very frustrating, difficult and time-consuming!

Marionettes can be safely packed away in a box or bag if you remember one simple rule. Twirl the puppet before placing it in the box. Hold the sticks in one hand and give the marionette a spin with the other. The strings now look all mixed up, but they aren't. Next roll the spun puppet up on the sticks, to keep the strings from untwirling. Now it can be carefully packed in a box or bag.

A good way to display your marionette is to take a piece of wood—nicely finished if possible—and mount small coat hooks on it. Hang one marionette from each hook as your collection grows.

Did You Know That...
The first marionettes were made in China. Chinese parents probably made them from dolls, and used strings to make the dolls move, to amuse their children.

Operating the Marionette: Basics

Marionettes can indeed be magical if they are manipulated well. The key to keep in mind is always to make their actions natural. Young puppeteers tend to keep their marionettes constantly moving, swinging or floating. Unfortunately, this distracts the audience from the plot or story. Try to eliminate all unnecessary action, and stick to clear, bold gestures, to keep the characters looking realistic.

Puppeteers' five basic rules are:

• Keep the marionette's feet on the floor of the stage—unless it's a character like Peter Pan or a witch. Otherwise, no flying!

• Keep the marionette facing the audience unless it's walking on or off stage, or interacting with another character.

• Always walk the marionettes in and out of the stage area—never have them fly out of the top of the scene as they're exiting.

• Have only one marionette moving at a time, with the others focussing on his actions.

• Strive for natural movements, or the audience will become more interested in the peculiar manipulation of the marionette than in the story.

Operating the Marionette: Actions

Now that the marionette is built, you'll want to be able to operate it easily and effectively. To begin, lay the operating sticks across the open palm of your left hand (or your right hand if you're left-handed). Then just thread your fingers among the strings so that the stick lies on your open hand.

Waving

Using your free hand, take the right-hand side of the red hand string about 5 cm (2 inches) down from the stick. Hold the string between your thumb and index finger. Jiggle your ring finger (third finger) against the string, below the thumb and index finger. The right hand of the marionette should be moving; the left hand should be still. Remember to keep the marionette's feet on the floor at all times! To wave the left hand, reverse these directions by taking the left-hand side of the red string.

Walking

Hold the marionette with your palm open, the sticks resting on top. Grasp the blue string on the right side about 7 cm (3 inches) down from the stick. Lift up on the string so that the knee of the marionette is lifted, in a natural-looking manner. The left leg will be straight. Now pull down on the same string until the left knee has been raised in the same way. Continue pulling up and down on the blue string in the same place, while you slowly move the stick forward. Voilà—your marionette is walking!

Sitting

To have your marionette sit down properly requires a bit of practice. Slowly walk it up to a marionette-size chair or couch. Turn the puppet around carefully, always keeping in mind a natural movement, so that its back is toward the seat. Slowly lower the sticks until the puppet is sitting on the chair. Watch that its back remains fairly straight, so that it looks natural.

Lying down

To have your marionette lie down on that same couch, continue from the sitting position. Carefully turn the puppet to one side as it is sitting. Lift the legs up onto the couch while gradually tipping the marionette backward to the lying down position. Jiggle the blue strings a little if the legs get stuck in the "knees bent" position. (Remember—never put your hand down into the stage area to adjust the marionette. It's a great temptation, but don't do it. You'll spoil the illusion.)

Taking a Bow

Hold the sticks as before. Grasp the yellow back string about 7 cm (3 inches) down from the sticks, and gradually lower the sticks. The yellow back string will be the only thing holding up the marionette, while the rest of the strings droop—and your marionette takes a bow!

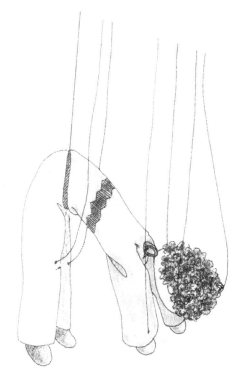

Kneeling

Hold the marionette as usual, on your open palm. Lower the sticks about 5 cm (2 inches) and move them slightly forward. The puppet should now be kneeling on both knees.

To have it kneel on one knee, hold it as usual again. Then take the blue string and make the puppet put one foot in front of the other. Lower the sticks about 5 cm (2 inches), again moving them slightly forward. The marionette should be kneeling on one knee. (Now the Prince can propose!)

Jumping

The technique for jumping is both easy and difficult. The easy part is that all you have to do is lift the sticks quickly to simulate jumping. The hard part is to make it look natural, but here are some hints. Try to keep the body level, bend the marionette's knees a bit before you lift up, and avoid swaying the body back and forth.

Pulling and Pushing Objects

Lean the marionette's body against an object, like a box, to push it. Avoid "hitting" the object with the marionette, because that will spoil the sense of a natural pushing action. Bend the marionette into the push a little, for added effect. Then move the marionette forward while another operator uses a string tied to the object, so both puppet and object move forward at the same time. Do just the reverse to make it appear that the marionette is pulling something.

Picking Up Objects

Moving an object in a scene can be accomplished with strings—just tie a string to the object. Then lower the marionette's hand to the object and bring the hand of the marionette up as you pull the object up with the string.

Dancing

Two marionettes dancing is fun to watch! It's possible to do if the strings are exactly the same length on both puppets. Hold the two marionettes in one hand, joining the sticks at the red string end. With the other hand grasp the two blue strings closest to you (one from each marionette), and pull and lift in a dancing rhythm. Turning the sticks so that the marionettes turn while dancing gives them the illusion of waltzing.

Red Ends Together

Magic Hat

A hat can be made to go up and down on a puppet's head using a string, too. When a clown makes a funny gesture, up goes his hat!

Opening a Box

A marionette can open a box quite easily if the lid of the box is rigged with a string. Imagine your marionette opening a birthday present, a pirate opening a treasure chest, kids looking in a box they found in Grandma's attic, a bank robber opening a suitcase full of money, and so on—just match the action to your script.

Passing Objects Between Marionettes

This is best left to the expert, but it can be accomplished with two keen novices and plenty of practice. Magnets do the trick! The object to be passed must be metallic, or have a piece of metal hidden inside it. A small metal nut or bolt, or a small magnet used for kitchen cupboards and found in a hardware store, is handy. The magnet in the hand the object is being passed **to** must be stronger than the magnet in the hand initiating the passing. The effect is very realistic.

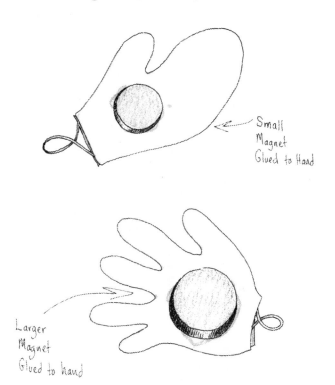

Small
Magnet
Glued to Hand

Larger
Magnet
Glued to hand

Passing Puppets During a Performance

Sometimes when a marionette has to cross over to the other side of the stage, it is not always possible for the operator of the marionette to cross over at the back of the stage, either because there are too many other people there, or because he or she can't move fast enough for the stage action. It is easier in this case to hand the marionette to the person who is on the correct side of the stage. He or she can hand it back to you again when your character returns to your side of the stage; or if not, sometimes trading marionettes mid-way through a scene is best. The transfer between puppeteers must never be detected by the audience—you have to complete the changeover very carefully. It's fun afterward if someone asks "Who was working Jack?", to say "When do you mean? I had him during the horse scene but Mary had him during the giant scene."

Other Gestures

Always strive for a natural effect while operating a marionette. For example, if a marionette is singing it could be swaying to the music and swaying its head. The black strings enable the puppet to nod its head from side to side. Simply tip the sticks back and forth from left to right, allowing one side of the head to tilt slightly one way, and then the other. Repeat the movement to the beat of the music.

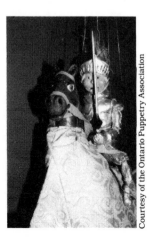

Courtesy of the Ontario Puppetry Association

Building the Stage

a) *Ultra-Simple Stage*

You will need:

- a very large cardboard box

- scissors

- paint and paintbrushes

Cut the bottom and the top off the box. Then cut out one panel, open it up and—voilà!—a stage that sits on the floor while the marionettes are operated from behind. The "wings" of the stage will curve forward.

Paint a little scenery on the background and you're all set. Don't worry that the audience can see the operators. In a few minutes they'll be fascinated by the actions of the marionettes, not the puppeteers. Or, if you'd prefer the puppeteers not be seen at all, tie a sheet to a line, and set it slightly forward of the back stage wall, so that it hides the operators but shows the stage.

b) Temporary Stage

You will need:

- a very large cardboard box, the kind a fridge or stove comes in

- the same materials as for the ultra-simple stage

For a slightly more professional, but still easy-to-make stage, cut the top off the box, but leave the bottom on. Leave the back on, too.

Cut a 60 × 60 cm (24 × 24 inch) opening from the lower front of the box, for the stage opening. Then cut the back down, to approximately 80 cm (30″) from the floor.

Paint the scenery on the inside back of the box. Then you can stand behind it, and operate the marionettes that are **within** the box. (Be sure to seat your audience directly in front of the stage opening, so they can see the marionettes clearly.)

Did You Know That...
Chinese puppets were made from the dried skin of sheep, water buffaloes, pigs and even certain kinds of fish.

c) Permanent Stage

You will need

- 2½ sheets of 6 mm (¼ inch) plywood

- 7.6 m (25 feet) of strapping or cleating (2.5 × 5.1 cm, or 1 × 2 inch)

- screwdriver and 60 2.5 cm (1 inch) screws

- keyhole saw, hand saw, auger or drill, scissors, adjustable wrench

- 6 6.3 cm (2½ inch) hinges; 36 nuts and bolts (2.5 cm or 1 inch long)

- 4 hook and eye screws plus 4 matching eyelets

- 76.2 cm (30-inch) curtain rod and brackets (length may vary, but should not exceed measurements above)

- 12 cup hooks

- (Optional) 91.4 cm or 36-inch dowel to use as a curtain rod for easy disassembling of the stage

- fabric for curtains, enough for a finished size of 76.2 cm wide × 66 cm long (30 inches wide × 26 inches long)

- curtain hooks (if you're using a rod) or curtain rings (if you're using a dowel)

- fluorescent light fixture about 46 cm (18 inches) long, and brackets

- sturdy bench, about 50 cm (20 inches) high

- paint and paintbrushes

- ruler and pencil

Saw 41 cm (16 inches) off the top of one full sheet of plywood to make a piece 122 × 203 cm (48 × 80 inches).

Saw this piece in half lengthwise to make two 61 × 101.5 cm (24 × 80 inch) pieces. These will be the stage sides or wings. Mark the top, bottom, inner and outer edges in pencil.

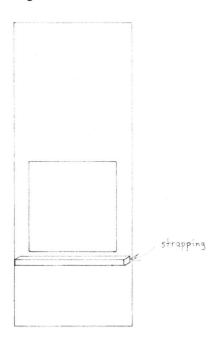

strapping

Saw 41 cm (16 inches) off both the top and one side of the second full sheet of plywood, to make one 81.3 × 203 cm (32 × 80 inch) piece. This will be the stage front. Mark the top, bottom and sides in pencil.

Cut a 61 × 61 cm (24 × 24 inch) hole in the stage front. The bottom of the opening should be 48.3 cm (19 inches) above the bottom edge of the plywood. Use an auger or drill until there's enough space for a keyhole saw to fit, then finish with a hand saw.

Cut a piece of strapping 76.2 cm (30 inches) long. Screw it onto the inside of the stage front, centred below the opening. The top edge of the strapping should be 47.6 cm (18¾ inches) from the bottom edge of the plywood. Screw from the front of the stage, into the strapping on the back. (The 5.1 cm or 2-inch side of the strapping attaches to the plywood. NOTE: This applies to all strapping that will be attached to the plywood pieces.)

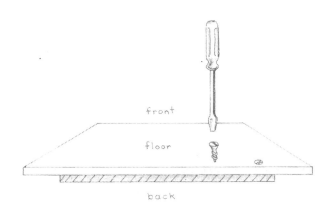

Cut a 41 × 122 cm (16 × 48 inch) piece from the remaining plywood, or from the half sheet. Measure in 20.3 cm (8 inches) from each edge of the top side. Draw a line to the outside bottom edge. Saw along this line. The resulting quadrilateral shape will form the stage floor. Mark the front, rear, left side and right side with pencil.

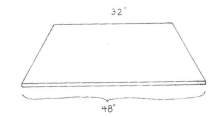

Cut a 111.8 cm (44-inch) piece of strapping. Centre the strapping on the longest floor edge, and have it jut out **below** the floor to form a 1.3 cm (½ inch) lip. Screw it on below the rear of the stage floor (from the top, through the plywood and into the strapping.)

Cut a 71.1 × 122 cm (28 × 48 inch) piece for the back wall of the stage from the half sheet of plywood. Mark the top, bottom, right side and left side with pencil.

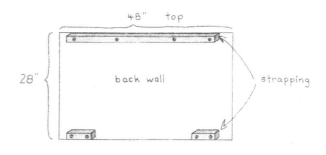

Cut a 116.8 cm (46-inch) piece of strapping and screw it onto the outside top edge of the back stage wall. (Screw through the plywood and into the strapping.)

Cut two 10 cm (4-inch) pieces of strapping. Screw them onto the lower back edge of the wall, 2.5 cm (1 inch) in from each side (through the plywood and into the strapping).

Cut two pieces of 35.6 cm (14-inch) strapping. Take one stage wing section. Screw one piece of strapping onto the inside of the wing, horizontally, so that the top of the piece of strapping is 47.6 cm (18¾ inches) from the bottom of the wing section. The outer edge of the strapping should be 43.2 cm (17 inches) from the inner edge of the wing. Leave a 1-cm (³⁄8 inch) gap. Then screw on the second piece of strapping directly above it. Repeat for the second wing. These gaps will

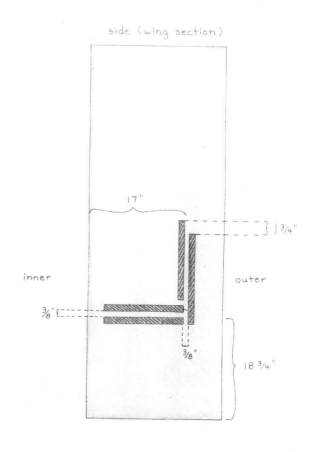

make grooves for the stage floor to slide into.

Cut two pieces of strapping 71.1 cm (28 inches) long. On one wing section, screw on a vertical piece of strapping. The piece of strapping, including the width of the strapping itself, should be 43.2 cm (17 inches) in from the inner edge of the wing. Leave a gap of 1 cm (³/₈ inch) and screw on the second piece of strapping behind the first, but place it 4.5 cm (1³/₄ inches) lower than the first.

Repeat for the second wing section. The gaps make grooves for the stage back to slide into, until it meets the lip on the back edge of the stage floor.

Screw a hook and eye into the top strapping at each side of the stage back. Place it in from the outer edge of the strapping, at a distance just slightly less than the length of the hook. Screw an eyelet into the side of the inner vertical strapping on each stage wing, near the top of the strapping.

Screw a hook and eye into the bottom piece of strapping at each side of the bottom edge of the stage back. Screw an eyelet into the outer vertical strapping on each wing, slightly higher than the hook and eye.

Attach the wings of the stage to the front piece with the six sets of hinges, three to each side. (Drill holes for the bolts. Insert the bolts from the front, and place nuts on the back. Tighten.) Stand the stage upright.

> HINT: At this time you'll need a helper to hold the stage while you slide in the remaining pieces. It won't be entirely steady until all pieces are together and attached.

Slide the stage floor, narrower end forward, into the groove between the pieces of horizontal strapping, until it meets the stage front. Be sure the lip of strapping is on the lower side. Adjust the two wings to meet the stage floor sides.

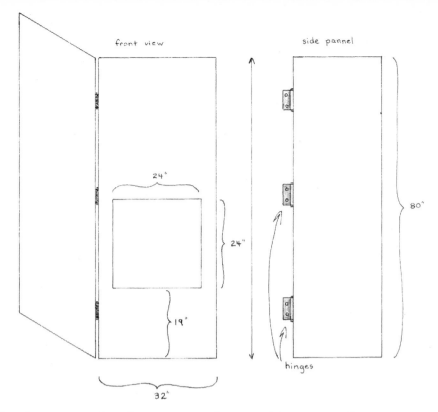

Slide the stage back section down the vertical grooves on the two wings, until it rests on the lip of strapping. Attach the hooks to the eyes at the top of the stage back, and also at the bottom.

(Optional) If the stage does not feel entirely firm, you can attach an 81.3 cm (32-inch) piece of 5.1 × 10.2 cm (2 × 4 inch) wood at the outside bottom edge of the stage front, to keep it from tipping forward. (Use shelf brackets.)

When the puppeteer stands on the bench behind the back wall, he or she should be able to see the stage floor. Test for height by lifting a marionette over the back wall and walking it across the stage.

Attach the light fixture on the inside of the stage front, above the opening, but with enough space to hang a curtain rod below (about 7.6 cm or 3 inches).

Hang the curtain rod below the light, using a bracket at each end, on the inside of the stage front. With some leftover material, make simple curtains to hang across the opening. Attach curtain rings at the top of the curtains, large enough to allow for easy opening and closing of the curtains.

(Optional) If you're using a dowel for a curtain rod, drill a hole in each wing, just above the level of the top of the stage opening, and slip the dowel through the two holes. The dowel is handy if you plan to fold up the stage frequently, since it slips out easily and allows for flatter folding, and the brackets for the curtain rod need not be removed each time you disassemble the stage.

Screw in cup hooks on the inside of the stage near the top edge, about 15 cm (6 inches) apart. Marionettes which are not being used in the present scene are stored here, on the sides and front, ready for immediate retrieval during the show. (They should be hung high enough to remain unseen from the front.)

Paint the stage exterior.

The stage can be folded down nearly flat, for easy storage, by detaching the hooks from the eyelets, sliding out the stage back, then the stage floor. (Use a helper at this time, since this is when the stage can tip over.) Then remove the dowel or the curtain rod, and the light fixture. Fold the wings inward towards the back.

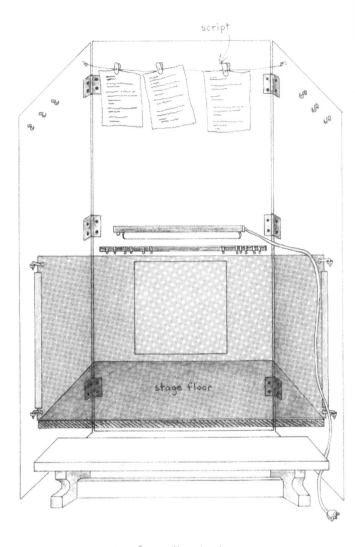

view from the back

NOTE: The stage floor will support marionettes, props and scenery, but don't let children walk on it, since the plywood may not be strong enough to support them.

Props

Some simple prop ideas follow—adapt them to suit the action in your own play.

Signposts

If your play includes a chase scene, add drama with a moveable direction sign, so that a villain can make the heroes run the wrong way! Here's the trick. Simply attach the sign to an unbent coat-hanger and lower it to the stage from the top. As the hero approaches, the puppet operator places the hand of the villain marionette on the sign, and another operator turns the coat-hanger from above at the same time, creating the illusion that the puppet has changed the direction of the sign.

Jack's Beanstalk

The illusion of the growing beanstalk in *Jack and the Beanstalk* can be created by the use of a coiled metallic spring toy (a slinky). Covering the toy with leaves of crêpe paper accomplishes the beanstalk effect.

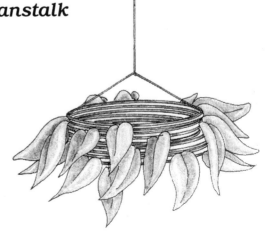

coathanger

While it's lying on the stage floor it simply looks like a pile of leaves. But as night falls the stalk begins to grow magically—a puppeteer or operator pulls up on the strings that have been attached to the toy, until it stands full grown.

Space Slide

Characters can swoop down into a scene through the use of a cardboard slide. They enter the scene from the top, then move down the slide to the stage floor. The mood is enhanced by adding a sound effect made by running a stick over a xylophone, from the top notes through to the bottom. The space slide idea can be effective for an explorer moving into a time warp, a character falling down a chute in a high-tech spaceship, and so on.

Did You Know That...
Pierrot is a famous French puppet created by George Sand. He always wears a traditional white satin costume, and is very sad and melancholy.

Tree or Flagpole

A tree or flagpole can be placed in a scene from above, using the same coat-hanger prop as the signpost, but attaching a tree made from construction paper to it. A marionette can then hide behind the tree, creating a 3-D effect, which adds to the simple painted background. An operator simply holds the tree from above until the scene changes.

Moving Props

The following idea can be adapted to a variety of props. Attach strings to the prop, and jerk them to the side, or from the top, to make the prop move when a character does something to it. Or, if you can only pull the string from the top, put an eyehook in the floor of the stage, near the wings. This way, when you pull **up** on the string, it will pull an object to the **side.** You can use the same idea to roll a car, a boat, or a bicycle along the floor of the stage. This can be handy if you aren't creating rolling scenery (see page 56) to go behind the marionettes.

All kinds of props can be temporarily attached to the marionette's hands for individual scenes. Pirates can carry swords, old people can lean on canes, a farmer can hoe crops, a teacher can carry a book. Characters can even pretend to eat food—pizza, sandwiches, and so on. The props can be made from papier-mâché, or any scaled-down models you can create. Use masking tape to attach the prop to the puppet, since it won't peel off paint when it's removed. Puppeteers can also be trained to use various objects on the stage as props—sitting at desks on chairs, riding in boats or cars, even swinging on a trapeze or riding a broomstick!

Scenery

The main point about scenery is to keep it fairly simple—audiences get bored during long scenery changes. For example, crumpled aluminum foil painted black, with subdued lighting, creates a spooky, mysterious cave for a villain—or a heavy metal rock scene!

Different sets suggesting a variety of locations can be created with a bit of imagination. Jail bars made of wool hanging from a metre stick or yardstick (or an unbent coathanger with tape over the sharp ends), and suspended at the front of a scene, make a wonderful prison. Villains have even been known to make an escape because the jail bars were made of red licorice!

Rolling Scenery
One of the most successful and effective scenery techniques is rolling scenery. The backdrop for each scene of the play is

painted on a long piece of heavy paper. The backdrop piece should be slightly longer and wider than the stage opening. (Be sure that everything drawn or painted on the rolling scenery is outlined with a thin black line, so that all details can be clearly seen by the audience.)

After it's dry, attach it to two metre sticks or yardsticks, one at each end. The paper is then placed in the stage and the scenery rolled along by two operators above, as each scene changes. When the scenery has been established for a scene, the operators can keep it from unwinding too early by pegging clothespins just inside the rolled-up ends—the same way you'd keep a poster from rolling up.

Normally the scenery would be rolled at the end of a scene while the curtains are drawn, but if the illusion of a walking marionette is desired then the scenery rolls along behind him or her, giving the audience the impression that the character is really walking—such as *The Paper Bag Princess* going through the burnt forests to find the dragon, or an explorer or hunter travelling through the jungle. Swimming or flying impressions can be created, too—a fish or submarine swimming through an underwater seascape, Tom Sawyer rafting down a river, a space explorer passing comets, meteors, planets and stars. The variety is as limitless as your imagination.

The Paper Bag Princess, by Robert Munsch. Published by Annick Press Ltd, Toronto, Canada. © 1980 Robert N. Munsch

Sound Effects

Sound effects can be recorded on tape and played during the performance—knocking on doors, telephones ringing, and so on. A xylophone produces excellent effects for fantasy or dream sequences—check out the sound effect for the Space Slide in the Props section on page 54.

Similarly, you can create and tape sound effects for other scenes. Use your ingenuity.

Some of the most effective sound effects have come from everyday occurrences that have been worked into the storyline of a marionette show. For example, cars and trucks starting up; household sounds such as dishes clashing, cutlery dropping on the floor, dogs barking, a cat's meow, telephone ringing, doorbell gong, taps dripping, etc. There are also plenty of opportunities outdoors; running water, traffic sounds, bird calls.

If you want assistance beyond the possibilities of your own environment, remember that many libraries have sound effect records to lend. This may help with rowdy crowd scenes, jumbo jet take offs, car chases, and so on.

And don't forget general sound effects that can make your play more realistic—the sound of horses' hooves, creaking chairs, squeaking doors on a haunted house, ticking time bombs, slamming doors, lightning and thunder (rattle a cookie sheet), trees rustling in the woods, animal noises in a barnyard, outer space noises, snapping branches.

Did You Know That...
The first marionettes in North America were probably native ones used in religious ceremonies.

Marionette Ideas for One or Two Puppeteers

Even if you don't want to write a play for your marionette to perform in, they can be fun to make and play with. Here are some simple ideas:

• A marionette can be made as a craft project, to be hung in your room or the family room, like a piece of art.

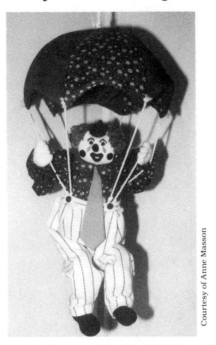

Courtesy of Anne Masson

• Select a song, poem, favourite book to perform. A record can serve as a soundtrack. Put it on and act it out.
Attach small musical instruments to your marionettes and have a concert. Rock songs work well when a cardboard guitar is glued onto a character. A keyboard is easily made out of a cardboard box. Add a few flashing lights and the show is ready to go on. If you prefer something in a more classical vein, make music stands from pieces of wood and wire. Violins and cellos can be cut out of cardboard. Just move the marionettes' hands as they're "playing" their instruments.

• Use a mirror and put on a show for yourself! Just place a mirror carefully on the floor, leaning against a chair or a wall. Then have the marionette perform. He or she can sing a song, play a guitar, and so on. When you've practised a lot, show someone else what you can do.

Ideas for Large Groups or a Class

Writing a Play

A day or so ahead of the play-writing session, post a list of the various elements of a story, to get children thinking about who they'd like the play to be about, what could happen to the characters, where it could take place, and so on:

- Characters
- Theme
- Plot
- Moral
- Setting
- Resolution
- Climax
- Conclusion

The first play-writing session should start with an informal brainstorming activity. Get as many ideas as you can, by using standard brainstorming techniques—that is, list everything the children say, and make no judgements. One child who offers something outrageous might trigger another child's creativity. A later process of elimination and voting will narrow the lists to a more manageable size.

If you are new to brainstorming with children, try some of the following loaded questions:

- Who will your story be about? (names, creatures, animals...)

- Will he or she have any friends? Any accomplices? Any sisters or brothers?

- Could he or she have any enemies?

- Where will the story take place? (town, house, cave, desert island, school...)

- Will the characters travel somewhere else? Where?

  (At this point you'll probably be having trouble recording names and places as fast as the children are spouting ideas!)

- Now, what's going to happen to your character(s)? Something good? Something bad? Something involving a friend or an enemy? Some event?

By now you'll have enough material to start selecting specific material. Take your first list—main characters—and tell the children they're going to vote several times, until **only one** main character remains. The first vote will probably leave about five favourite characters. Erase the rest—they've been eliminated. Now the children get to vote again for the remaining characters. Keep eliminating the character with the lowest number of votes until a single main character remains. Now you have your lead character.

Courtesy of the Ontario Puppetry Association

Go back to the second list, the one with the main character's friends or accomplices, and repeat the voting procedure to arrive at the main character's sidekick or partner. Sometimes, depending on the children, the time of year—even the weather outside!—it's necessary to pause and come back to the process later. The wait helps give the children time to come up with other ideas for the next session. (I've written plays with some children in one morning; with others I've taken three days or more, in brief sessions each day.)

You can easily introduce a topic for a suitable plot, as well as a theme. Children can be encouraged towards a play involving a science theme they're currently studying, or perhaps they'll be willing to incorporate a seasonal or local school event into their play. Middle-grade children can be particularly moral—they usually come up with a good guy and a bad guy. You might try to steer them away from too much violence by saying that the play will be put on for younger children—kindergartners make a great audience!—and you wouldn't want to scare them.

After you have decided on a plot or story line, discuss some major event that will happen in the play. This can form either the main conflict or become the climax—some kind of trouble for the main characters, a big decision, good news, bad news, a funny event, and so on.

Did You Know That...
Howdy Doody was a famous marionette of the 1950's. Buffalo Bob Smith created him as one of the most complicated of all types of puppets. He appeared on a popular 50's television programme.

Now all the children have to do is find a way for the characters to solve the problem, or make the decision, and voilà—their very own play. It's a good idea to keep it fairly short. You'll want to leave the audience wanting more, instead of wondering if the play will ever end!

All through the brainstorming process, as you clarify the characters, plot and action, the children can consider any special effects, props or sound effects that might be desired. Rolling scenery is always a very popular and effective trick, so be sure to include a scene in which the characters are walking or riding somewhere, with the scenery rolling behind them.

Punch and Judy

Did You Know That...
The famous British puppet, Punch, has become international. This muddle-headed but good-hearted puppet character is called *Karagoz* in Turkey, *Hanswurst* in Germany and *Petroushka* in Russia.

Writing Dialogue with Children

After the general story-writing time, the actual writing of dialogue begins. One easy method is to divide the play into small segments and hand out sheets requiring dialogue for a specific scene or part of a scene. Younger children in particular will have difficulty writing dialogue for a whole play—to say nothing of you having to choose the best piece of dialogue from several writers. Therefore, it's better if you get a child to focus on one scene. Then another child will write another part, and in the end nearly everyone will have written a few lines of the play. For example: Using "The Paper Bag Princess" Characters: Paper Bag Princess, Dragon, Prince Ronald.

Write some dialogue for this scene:

When the princess tricks the dragon into flying around the world, how would she get him to do it? What would he say?

Princess: _____ .

Dragon: _____ .

Princess: _____ .

Dragon: _____ .

Princess: _____ .

Dragon: _____ .

Princess: _____ .

Dragon: _____ .

Using this method solves several problems. The children have something specific to write about, so you can stop the brainstorming process for awhile and write actual dialogue for the scenes they have created so far. The plot may change slightly during this stage of writing, but not nearly as much as during the initial brainstorming activity. Always remember that the play is for the children themselves, so don't worry if it sounds a bit corny to you. Other children will love it, and more importantly, if you tamper with the dialogue too much, it won't be "their play" anymore. Children will become very attached to the parts they've written, and swell with pride each time "their line" is heard during rehearsals and performances, so you'll want to leave it the way they wrote it. All you really need to do is watch out for sensitive subject matter (i.e. stereotyping) and violence.

Courtesy of the Ontario Puppetry Association

Did You Know That...
The Russians used marionettes in their "Vertep" plays. They were named after the three-storied booth that formed their stage. They first performed in churches, and later at fairs at Christmas.

What Type of Performance?

When the play has been rehearsed sufficiently, it's time to arrange for the performance. The method of presentation depends on a variety of factors. The first thing to consider is how comfortable the children might be at putting on a live show. If you have concerns about that, here are some suggestions.

Videotaped Performance

Sometimes having a helper come in and videotape the performance can solve a multitude of problems. A video can be stopped in the middle of a scene and re-recorded if a problem arises. This is a good idea for rehearsal purposes whether or not you decide to show the video to the audience. Sometimes a combination of video, plus a particularly popular—and simple—scene performed live, may be more appropriate.

Taping the Dialogue Soundtrack

Because of the complexity of manipulating the marionettes in the close quarters backstage, it is important for the smooth running of a performance for the puppeteers to have as little to worry about as possible. For this reason a pre-recorded soundtrack works very well. The fears about forgetting lines is eliminated, and producing the soundtrack allows for more children to become involved in the preparation of the show. If a large group or a whole class is creating the play, one group can be working on the soundtrack while another is rehearsing with marionettes, and still another is creating props and scenery. Basically the script is rehearsed, and then recorded on tape.

Since the dialogue can usually be spoken much faster than the puppets are able to move, be sure to leave enough time for the marionette to accomplish the action he or she is speaking of. (For example, in *The Paper Bag Princess,* Elizabeth says, "Is it true that you can fly around the world in just ten seconds?" and the dragon proudly does it. Be sure to leave enough time for the dragon to exit to the right, be handed around the back of the stage, and be brought in again from the left, before Elizabeth speaks to him again. If the speakers work with the rehearsing marionette operators, they'll get a good idea of how much time to leave.)

During the actual performance, a child could be holding the tape recorder and viewing the performance, so that if some action takes longer than expected, or a mishap occurs which delays the action, he or she can hit the pause button, and resume the tape when the operators are ready to proceed.

Space must also be left on the tape in between scenes to allow for scenery changes and prop additions, the entrance of new marionettes, and so on. You might even experiment with two tape recorders—one for the actual dialogue, one for theme music to play during scene changes or intermissions. Theme music helps tie the show together. Use it at the beginning of the play, like an overture, and at the closing of the show as the audience is leaving.

Live Performance

Some classes may wish to opt for a totally live performance, however, they may wish to experiment with a taped performance first. Some of the following hints should keep the play moving along smoothly if you decide to perform live.

• Practise, practise, practise. You can never rehearse too much.

• Use a simple play, one that avoids too many scenery changes and props. A simple show well done looks much better than a complicated one with several unavoidable goofs.

• Post a copy of your script on the inside front wall of the stage, so it can be referred to throughout the performance. Mark the script with different coloured pens showing props, special effects, cues for entrance and for rolling the scenery, and so on.

• Keep a table backstage, behind the operators' bench. Keep all your props and other necessities on this table in an organized fashion. You can separate props needed for various scenes into different areas. Your emergency kit (see page 76) should be here too.

• If possible, have someone entertain the audience during the scenery changes. (I used to do magic tricks!) That way the audience isn't allowed to get bored while the scenery is being changed, and they appreciate the extra entertainment. A song or a poetry recitation can be helpful here.

• Put curtains up along both sides of the stage, so the audience can't peek in and see what you're doing! Especially if you have many cast members, there's not much room back there, and some people will have to stand in the wings.

• Remember to keep one or two marionettes in reserve, in case you drop one by mistake and can't untangle its strings. It's helpful to take a piece of distinguishable clothing, or a prop, off the tangled marionette and put it on the new one, so the audience will still recognize the character.

• Ignore minor problems that might occur. Most of the time the audience will be unaware of a goof unless a big deal is made of it. Long pauses while you try to figure out how to remedy something are worse than just carrying on.

Courtesy of the Ontario Puppetry Association

Lights...Camera...Action...
Preparing for the Show

Co-operation is the key in the cramped quarters of the backstage area. Each scene must be carefully choreographed as to who stands where and who holds which marionette when. Here are some hints for a smoothly flowing performance.

• Preparation is very important—you really can't rehearse too much!

• Tape a copy of the script about 30 cm (12 inches) above the light on the inside of the front of the stage. It's a handy reference if you forget lines; or if you're using a taped soundtrack, use it to remind yourself of stage directions, and so on.

Getting Ready for the Audience

By the time you're into rehearsals, many people will be aware of your project and will be wondering when the show will actually emerge. An official announcement is a great way to begin, since it generates excitement and enthusiasm among the players and the audience. A sign-up sheet for those interested is recommended, so that the audience will not be too large. Since the stage area is fairly small, a limited number of children can see the play at one time. A classroom is generally the best size of room to use— anything much larger results in problems with the audience being able to see or hear clearly.

Marquis

At the door of the room where the performance will be held, a marquis, similar to those near the door of a movie theatre or playhouse, can be displayed. Drawings or pictures of the stars of the show, and curiosity provoking questions, can be scattered among photographs of key scenes.

Decorate the front of the stage. You can paint it, or use it to display the title of the play. Large letters cut out of contrasting coloured paper work well.

Courtesy of the Ontario Puppetry Association

Making Invitations

Another job for those children not directly involved in rehearsals is to make invitations for VIP's, inviting them to come to the play. Children can design a cover using drawings of scenes from the play, and provide necessary information on the inside. For a school setting, I always sent a "times available" list for other teachers to sign. That way you don't assign them an inappropriate time such as a gym or library period. When the responses are returned, have the children write an invitation including the time the teacher has already chosen. This serves as a handy reminder on that teacher's desk, too.

The Stars Behind the Marionettes

It's important to post a list of credits somewhere in the room. List every single job—no matter how small—and make sure that every child has his or her name included at least once on the page.

CREDITS

Marionette #1
   Name:

   Built by:

   Voice by:
   (Child who read the part)

   Puppeteer:
   (Child who operated the marionette)

Marionette #2
   Name:

   Built by:

   Voice by:
   (Child who read the part)

   Puppeteer:
   (Child who operated the marionette)

Marionette #3
   Name:

   Built by:

   Voice by:
   (Child who read the part)

   Puppeteer:
   (Child who operated the marionette)

Extra voices:

Props:

Music by:

Soloist:
  (piano, chimes, xylophone, and so on)

Sound Effects:

Understudies:

Scenery Operators:

Title Design:

Written and created by:

Scenery Painters:

Director:

Assistant Director:

Stage built by:

Costumes by:

During the Performance

Backstage

The standard rules and techniques for producing any show naturally apply to a marionette show as well. Silence backstage is hard to accomplish because of the amount of co-operation necessary between puppeteers, and the limited space. Opening and closing the curtains slowly and evenly can make the show appear professional. The key is to expect the unexpected and try to make the show look good no matter what might be happening backstage. Be prepared for a broken string on your main character, tangled strings, a missing prop, a puppeteer losing his/her balance on the bench, and so on. Don't let this scare you off—all of these "disasters" have happened to me, and the audience never even knew! Remember, the important thing is to have fun. "Disasters," of whatever variety, are part of the show.

Reminders for Puppeteers During the Show

• Be sure to make the sound track loud and clear.

• Keep very quiet backstage, since background noise may spoil the illusion.

• Hold tight to the sticks of your marionette. It is very embarrassing to have a puppet fall out of your hands! Never let your hands show in the stage area, or the illusion will be spoiled. People really forget there are operators behind the stage if you do it right.

• Keep an emergency kit handy. Include tools (hammer, screwdriver, nails, nuts, pliers, scissors), a needle, thread or string, tape, hooks, glue, wire, and pins. It's a good idea to include an extra couple of marionettes similar to the stars, so that in a crisis (such as dropping the marionette into the stage area and the strings getting all tangled up) another marionette can be substituted.

• Keep smiling and have fun!

Follow-Up and Reinforcement

The possibilities for follow-up activities after you've put on your performance are limitless. Children generally love to evaluate something they have done, and the results can be quite enlightening. To have children comment that they felt proud when their marionette was finished gives the entire unit a new sense of worth. You're also given a greater indication of the abilities of individual students by asking about "the best part in making a marionette" or "the hardest thing about putting on the show." Answers such as, "Sewing the bodies was hardest for me," or "The head kept falling off," or "I felt happy," indicate the relative successes and limitations of the participants. Invariably there is a sense of pride when their work—having taken several weeks—is finally completed.

Here's a sample questionnaire you might use to check out various students' responses.

★★★

WE PUT ON A MARIONETTE SHOW!

1) The best part about making a marionette is _____
_____
_____ .

2) The hardest part about making a marionette is _____
because _____
_____ .

3) While we were making the marionette I felt _____
_____
_____ .

4) The puppet I made was supposed to be the character ___ .
   I made the character because _____
_____
_____ .

5) When my marionette was finished I felt _____
_____
_____ .

6) My part(s) in the show were _____
_____ .

7) The audience thought _____
_____ .

8) The best part of the show was _____
_____ .

9) One funny or unexpected thing that happened during the
   show was _____
_____
_____ .

★ ★ ★

Button making

If you have access to a button-making machine, this can be a great incentive for completing the marionette project. Buttons can be designed, drawn, and sent to a button-making shop, or the students might even be able to participate in making the buttons on the machine.

Marionette Sketching

Sketches can be made of the main character in the play, or a student's favourite marionette character, or his or her own marionette. Oil pastels are a good medium because their bright colours show up well on bulletin boards or hallways, but other media can work well, too.

Filmstrip Stories

Some school boards offer a filmstrip making facility, usually at the board office. Simply get specifics from the technician about the size needed, and have children illustrate and describe each step in the process, from making their marionettes to performing the play. (The text is generally placed at the bottom of the picture.)

Video

If you're really ambitious, try recording your entire marionette project on a video. Children will enjoy interviewing the performers, the scenery creators, the prop artists, the sound effect and lighting technicians as they prepare for the show—the possibilities are endless, and the behind-the-scenes angle will fascinate other children.

Behind-the-Scenes Classroom Books

Children love to write classroom books—that is, a book written and illustrated by the students themselves about something they have accomplished. If you have a camera, or you can persuade a volunteer to help, taking photographs of the children during each phase of the project (puppet making, scenery painting, and so on) provides excellent incentive motivation for a whole language arts project, which can continue long after the marionettes have been completed. "Tell me what **you** are doing in this photo" will motivate even the most reluctant writer. A "how-to" book or scrapbook can also serve as inspiration for next year's puppeteers. You'll find that children will invariably return to reread "their" book—even several years later!

I would love to hear about your experiences.

Dear Anne Masson,

Guess what? I've finished my marionette and it looks terrific! I made a _____ .

It looks _____ .

The best part about making a marionette is _____
_____ .

I had a hard time doing _____ .

Let me tell you something about me. I am _____ years old. I live in _____ . I like _____ .

Please write a letter back to me—I love to get letters from authors! Here's my address: _____
_____
_____

Here's a picture (or drawing) of my marionette, for your collection.

Sincerely,

Send your letter to:
Anne Masson
c/o ANNICK PRESS
15 Patricia Avenue
Willowdale, Ontario
M2M 1H9

THE PAPER BAG PRINCESS

A marionette play by Anne Masson

adapted from the story by Robert Munsch

Curtains remain closed while a voice-over announcer introduces the story. Music is heard in the background.

ANNOUNCER: Elizabeth was a beautiful princess. She lived in a castle and had expensive princess clothes. She was going to marry a prince named Ronald. Unfortunately, a dragon smashed her castle, burned all her clothes with his fiery breath, and then carried off Prince Ronald. Elizabeth decided to chase the dragon and get Ronald back. She looked everywhere for something to wear, but the only thing she could find that was not burnt was a paper bag.

Curtains open and Elizabeth enters wearing her paper bag clothes.

ANNOUNCER: So she put on the paper bag and followed the dragon.

Roll scenery behind her as Elizabeth walks along. The scenery is painted with burnt forests and horses' bones. There is a road down the middle.

ANNOUNCER: It was easy to follow the dragon because he left a trail of burnt forests and horses' bones. Finally Elizabeth came to a cave with a large door that had a huge knocker on it.

Loud knocks are heard. A dragon peeks out his head.

DRAGON: Well, a princess! I love to eat princesses, but I have already eaten a whole castle today. I am a very busy dragon. Come back tomorrow.

Dragon slams the door. Slamming sound effect. Elizabeth knocks again. Sound effect: three loud knocks.

DRAGON *(more irritated voice):* Go away. I love to eat princesses, but I have already eaten a whole castle today. I am a very busy dragon. Come back tomorrow.

ELIZABETH: Wait. Is it true that you are the smartest and fiercest dragon in the whole world?

DRAGON: Yes.

ELIZABETH: Is it true that you can burn up ten forests with your fiery breath?

DRAGON: Oh, yes.

Dragon turns offstage and a huge fiery sound effect is heard.

ELIZABETH: Wow! You just burned up fifty forests!

Dragon turns offstage and another huge fiery breath is heard.

ELIZABETH: Magnificent! There go another hundred forests!

One tiny poof of air is heard. Dragon appears, very tired, lying on the stage. His voice is tiny.

DRAGON: I haven't even got enough fire left to cook a meatball.

ELIZABETH: Dragon, is it true that you can fly around the world in just ten seconds?

DRAGON: Why yes. Watch me!

Dragon runs out stage right. Puppeteers lift him out and put him back in, stage left, and he enters from the left, all tired out.

ELIZABETH: Fantastic! Do it again!

Repeat dragon's exit and entrance, taking a longer time. This time he falls completely asleep when he arrives back on stage.

Elizabeth whispers towards dragon.

ELIZABETH: Hey, dragon.

Elizabeth walks over to the dragon and lifts up his ear, and yells.

ELIZABETH: Hey, dragon.

Elizabeth walks right over the dragon and opens the door to the cave. Enter Prince Ronald, whining.

PRINCE RONALD: Elizabeth, you are a mess! You smell like ashes, your hair is all tangled and you are wearing a dirty old paper bag. Come back when you are dressed like a real princess.

ELIZABETH: Ronald, your clothes are really pretty and your hair is very neat. You look like a real prince, but you are a bum!

ANNOUNCER: They didn't get married after all.

Curtains close. Introductory music is played again as the audience leaves.

Staging Hints for *The Paper Bag Princess*

Rolling Scenery

Make rolling scenery as per page 56. The left end (120–150 cm or 4–5 feet) is painted with burned forests and horses' bones. Then add the entrance to the cave, which includes a large door frame and a door with a large knocker.

Sound effects

Choose some classical music as an introductory piece. Some of the sound effects, such as the three loud knocks, can be done live, but you may want to tape the slamming door sound. Also, it's best to tape the sound of the dragon's huge fiery breath—use four or five voices all at once to achieve the right sound. (You need to face the dragon offstage as you do this sound effect, since it would be very difficult to create an effective fire-breathing effect onstage.)

Character hints

The dragon should be very fierce. See if you can make some rather floppy ears (not too big) so that Elizabeth can actually lift up the dragon's ear when she calls out to him. The fabric should be fairly light, or you can use the "lifting prop" idea .

Elizabeth: Use a real paper bag to make the dress. Have it torn a bit, and coloured dark at the edges to appear singed.

If you want to show her before she gets singed, you might want to use two marionettes for her role. At the start of the play, as the announcer is beginning, you can walk Elizabeth #1 onto the stage dressed as a usual princess. Before the announcer gets to "...a dragon smashed her castle..." you have to get her off the stage and then get the paper bag Elizabeth ready to enter.

ADDITIONAL RESOURCES

Books
Linda Williams Aber. *Hey, Gang! Let's Put on a Show!* (Instructor, 1987)

Linda Lang Aikenhead. *Mask & Melody; Drama & Music for Canadian Schools* (Thrice yearly periodical)

Shari Lewis, *Making Easy Puppets* (Dutton, 1958, 1960, 1967)

Violet Philpott & Mary Jean McNeil. *The Knowhow Book of Puppets* (Usborne, 1975)

Associations and Guilds
Canada
Association Québécoise des Marionnettistes, Case Postale 7, Succ. Delorimier, Montréal, Québec H2H 2N6
Téléphone: (514) 526-0370

Ontario Puppetry Association,
The Puppet Centre, 171 Avondale Ave., Willowdale, Ont. M2N 2V4
Telephone: (416) 222-9029

Vancouver Puppetry Guild,
4128 Sunset Blvd., North Vancouver, British Columbia V7R 3Y9
Telephone: (604) 987-3725

United States
Puppeteers of America, Inc.
Membership Office
5 Cricklewood Path
Pasadena, CA 91107-1002

Fellowship of Christian Puppeteers
7659 Rockfalls Road
Richmond, VA 23225

American Puppetmakers Assoc.
41 Washington Place
East Rutherford, NJ 07073

Magazines
The Puppetry Journal
(Published quarterly by Puppeteers of America)
George Latshaw, Editor
8005 Swallow Drive
Macedonia, OH 44056

Laugh*Makers
Variety Arts Magazine for Family & Kidshow Entertainers
Bob Gibbons, Publisher
4782 Streets Drive/Box 160
Syracuse, NY 13215

Anne Masson's interest in marionettes was sparked in 1962 when her grandfather returned from Mexico with a guitar playing stringed puppet. Soon the whole family was treated to shows performed by Anne and her two sisters.

This quickly grew into a marionette club with Anne and her friends producing fund raising shows for charity. As a present her father built them a "real" stage out of plywood; the same one that Anne uses in classrooms today!

For the past 20 years Anne has demonstrated the magic of marionettes to countless numbers of students, community groups and teachers. In addition, they have come in handy in her own teaching career. Marionettes have appeared in math class, art, science, physical education and reading.

Anne currently lives in a small town north of Toronto where she divides her time between making marionettes, marionette demonstrations and teaching.